Pharaoh Khufu *Born in 2589 B.C., Khufu was the son of the great pyramid builder Pharaoh Sneferu and Sneferu's wife, Hetepheres. Khufu reigned for about 24 years, during which he built the Great Pyramid of Giza. After Khufu's death in 2566 B.C., his son, Khafre, built a smaller pyramid next to his father's, eventually completing the last of the famous pyramids at Giza.*

Pharaoh Sneferu *The father of Pharaoh Khufu, Sneferu ruled ancient Egypt for about 24 years. This pharaoh was responsible for the building of the first true pyramid, the* Red *(or* Northern*) Pyramid. Due to its stability, it was the model for all the main pyramids at Giza. It also served as Sneferu's final resting place.*

Pharaoh Narmer *He is believed to have been a ruler of the First Dynasty (3050–2890 B.C.). Evidence of his existence has been found in various parts of Egypt, but it is not clear how he ruled. Theories suggest that he and the legendary King Menes are the same person.*

Queen Meritetes *Daughter of Pharaoh Sneferu and wife of Pharaoh Khufu. One of the pyramids of Giza is thought to have been built for her as her final resting place. She lived through the reigns of the Pharaohs Sneferu, Khufu, and Khafre.*

Queen Hetepheres *Hetepheres was the wife of Pharaoh Sneferu and mother of Pharaoh Khufu. She was buried in Dahshur, but her tomb was raided shortly afterward. Her remains have never been found.*

School Specialty.
Publishing

Copyright © ticktock Entertainment Ltd. 2006 First published in Great Britain in 2006 by ticktock Media Ltd., Unit 2, Orchard Business Centre, North Farm Road, Tunbridge Wells, Kent, TN2 3XF. This edition published in 2006 by School Specialty Publishing, a member of the School Specialty Family. Send all inquiries to School Specialty Publishing, 8720 Orion Place, Columbus, OH 43240.

Hardback ISBN 0-7696-4708-1   Paperback ISBN 0-7696-4692-1
1 2 3 4 5 6 7 8 9 10 TTM 10 09 08 07 06
Printed in China.

CONTENTS

THE COUNTRY OF EGYPT 4
• *Lower and Upper Egypt* • *Unification* • *King Narmer*
• *The first pyramids* • *Ancient Egyptian life and interest in the pyramids*

THE LIFE OF A PHARAOH 8
• *Many servants* • *A living god* • *Annual floods* • *Pleasing the gods*
• *Pharaoh Sneferu* • *Birth of Khufu* • *Death of Sneferu*

KHUFU'S BIG PLAN 14
• *Khufu's pyramid* • *Plans are made* • *Gathering workers*
• *Finding a site* • *The religious ceremony* • *Work begins*

TRANSPORTING THE MATERIALS 22
• *Skilled workers* • *Shipping the stones* • *The building site* • *Injuries*
• *Workers' spare time* • *Passages and vents* • *Laying the limestone*
• *Decorating and painting* • *Burying a boat*

DEATH OF A PHARAOH 38
• *Death of Khufu* • *Mummification* • *Transport by boat*
• *The Opening of the Mouth* • *Khufu's resting place* • *Grave robbers*
• *The pyramid today* • *Pyramid complex* • *A series of chambers*

TIMELINE & DID YOU KNOW? 44

GLOSSARY 46

INDEX 48

THE COUNTRY OF EGYPT

The great civilization of ancient Egypt grew from farming communities that settled along the Nile River. They relied on the Nile's flooding to make the soil fertile, allowing farmers to grow their crops. Before Egypt was ruled by kings, there was continual conflict between different parts of Egypt. Once King Narmer united Lower and Upper Egypt, Egypt became more peaceful, and the country prospered.

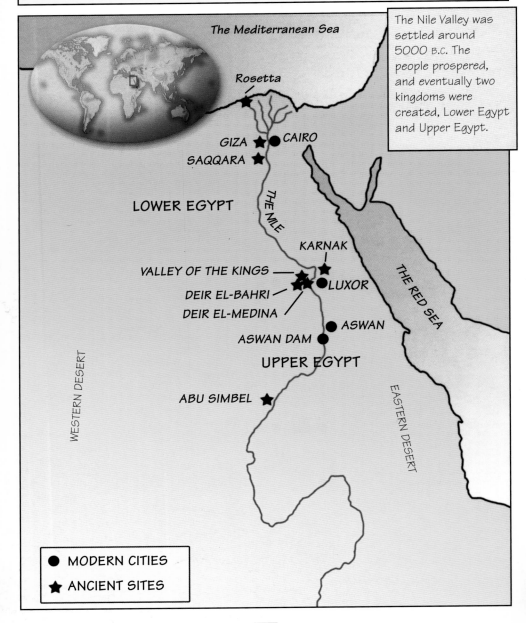

The Nile Valley was settled around 5000 B.C. The people prospered, and eventually two kingdoms were created, Lower Egypt and Upper Egypt.

The Mediterranean Sea

Rosetta

GIZA ★ ● CAIRO

SAQQARA ★

LOWER EGYPT

THE NILE

KARNAK

VALLEY OF THE KINGS — ★ ★ ● LUXOR

DEIR EL-BAHRI —

DEIR EL-MEDINA /

ASWAN ● ASWAN

ASWAN DAM ●

UPPER EGYPT

THE RED SEA

WESTERN DESERT

EASTERN DESERT

ABU SIMBEL ★

● MODERN CITIES

★ ANCIENT SITES

Around 3000 B.C., the two kingdoms of ancient Egypt were unified by King Narmer. He conquered Lower Egypt and began the reign of the pharaohs.

Narmer made himself the first king of Egypt. Under his rule, Egypt began to flourish. All of the rulers that followed him continued to make Egypt a powerful kingdom.

At last, we can have some peace between the two kingdoms. Now, we can get on with our farming.

Can you see who that is? It's King Narmer. I've heard that he is traveling through all of the lands that he has conquered.

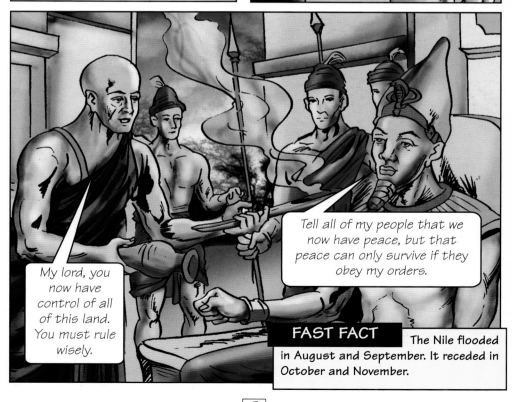

My lord, you now have control of all of this land. You must rule wisely.

Tell all of my people that we now have peace, but that peace can only survive if they obey my orders.

FAST FACT The Nile flooded in August and September. It receded in October and November.

The first pyramid was built about 500 years after King Narmer brought the two kingdoms together. It was built by King Djoser as a tomb for him and his family.

Later, my son. We have a lot of work to do first.

Father, can we go and see the tombs where our kings are buried? I've heard that they are so high you cannot climb to the top.

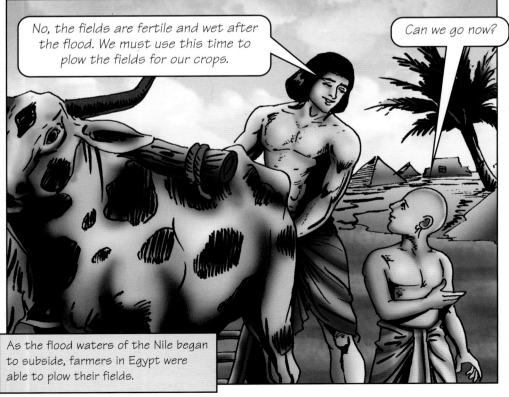

No, the fields are fertile and wet after the flood. We must use this time to plow the fields for our crops.

Can we go now?

As the flood waters of the Nile began to subside, farmers in Egypt were able to plow their fields.

Although the Egyptians had plows, they had to scatter the seeds on their fields by hand. It was hard work and took a long time to do.

Father, when we have finished, can we go and see the pyramids?

We have to scatter these seeds and then gather some more food.

Father, I can see the pyramids from up here.

Good, now gather as many figs as you can from the tree, my son.

The ancient Egyptians did not just rely on crops for their food. They also gathered food that was growing wild.

After the fields had been plowed and the seed had been planted, there was less work for the farmers to do.

There! You have worked hard, and now we can see the pyramids.

They're so big! They must have taken years to build!

THE LIFE OF A PHARAOH

The pharaohs were not just the rulers of ancient Egypt. They were seen as living gods with a special link to the gods that they worshipped. The daily life of a pharaoh followed a strict schedule.

The pharaoh was washed by a servant twice a day.

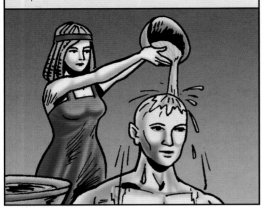

He was dressed by another servant.

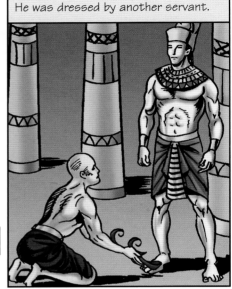

He met with his advisors.

For special occasions, the pharaoh had to wear a fake beard.

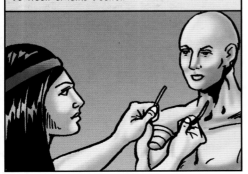

The pharaoh was seen as a living god. Religious ceremonies were a part of the pharaoh's everyday life.

The floods are nearly here. The pharaoh will pray for the waters to come.

If Thoth and Horus are with us, then the river will rise.

The gods and goddesses of ancient Egypt were given offerings as a way to gain their favor.

Khnum, guardian of the Nile, I offer you this food to bring the flood to Egypt.

FAST FACT As well as picking figs themselves, the ancient Egyptians also trained monkeys to pick them.

Around 2500 B.C., King Sneferu began the fourth dynasty of the Egyptian kingdom created by Narmer. Sneferu was a powerful king who conquered lands all around Egypt. He also wanted to make sure that Egypt remained powerful after his death.

My lord, you must have a son. Then, your power can be carried on for many years.

Keeping my kingdom together is my greatest wish. We must make sure that peace continues in Egypt after my death.

One day, Sneferu's wife, Hetepheres, had news for him.

I am expecting a child.

Good. Now my dynasty will remain safe.

A son. I have a son. I shall name him Khufu.

Because Khufu was such an important baby, both Sneferu and Hetepheres wanted to make sure that their gods would bless Khufu. They arranged for a special ceremony in a temple.

We call on the gods to protect this boy, Khufu. Make him grow, prosper, and one day rule this great land with wisdom and strength.

As Khufu grew, he began to learn all of the things a pharaoh needs to know. While his days were busy, he was also allowed some time to play with friends.

You must learn your lessons well. One day, you will rule all of this land.

ARCHERY

WRESTLING

FIGHTING WITH STICKS

PLAYING WITH TOY SOLDIERS

PLAYING WITH A BALL

READING AND WRITING

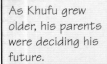
As Khufu grew older, his parents were deciding his future.

My lord, your son is nearly 15 years old. You know what he must do.

Yes, I know. I will tell him.

Sneferu found his son and told him what had been decided.

Khufu, you are now old enough to be married.

Yes, father. I will obey your command.

Hetepheres then spoke to Meritetes, the girl chosen to be Khufu's bride.

I am honored that you have chosen me. I will go and find Khufu now.

Khufu! Your mother has just spoken to me. We are to marry.

You will make a worthy queen, Meritetes.

Meritetes and Khufu were married in a ceremony watched by Hetepheres and Sneferu.

I call on Hathor, the goddess of love, and on Thoth, the god of wisdom, to bless this marriage and to make our kingdom stronger.

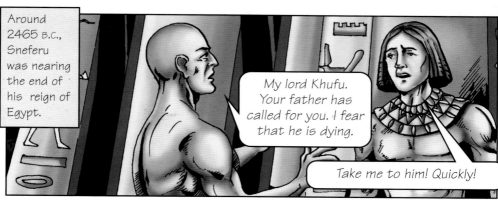

Around 2465 B.C., Sneferu was nearing the end of his reign of Egypt.

My lord Khufu. Your father has called for you. I fear that he is dying.

Take me to him! Quickly!

Father. I am here.

The time is coming when I shall meet the gods.

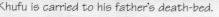

Khufu is carried to his father's death-bed.

Sneferu died. Khufu had been ready for this moment for many years. Now, he was pharaoh of all Egypt.

Your father has died. Now, you must rule this land as wisely as you can.

The body of Sneferu was carried to the pyramid that he had built at Dahshur.

FAST FACT During his lifetime, Sneferu built more pyramids than Khufu.

KHUFU'S BIG PLAN

After Sneferu's death, Khufu decided to build a great pyramid to honor his father. Building a pyramid required a lot of planning even before the first stones were laid. It not only needed workers, but also experts such as architects and skilled stonemasons.

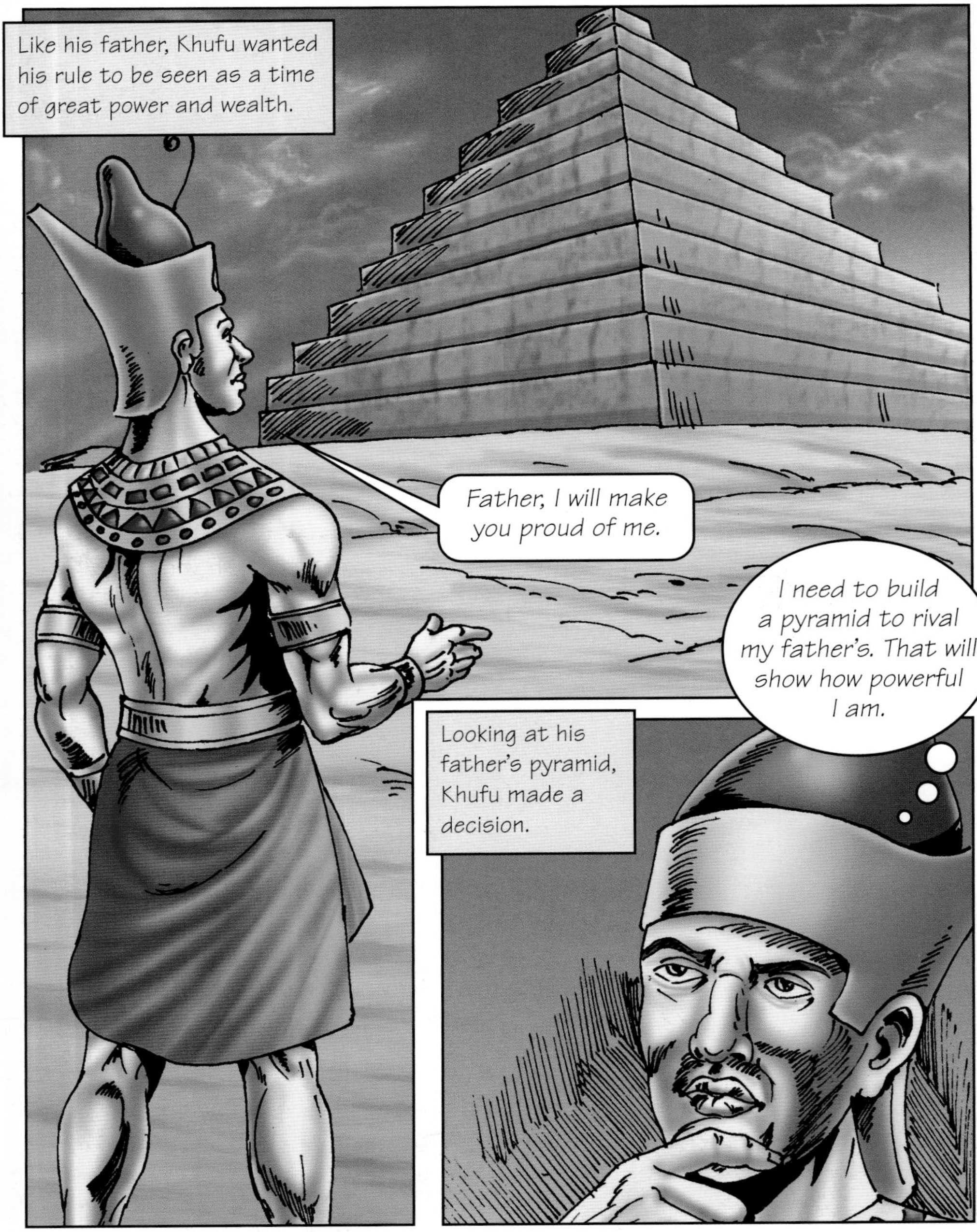

Like his father, Khufu wanted his rule to be seen as a time of great power and wealth.
Father, I will make you proud of me.
Looking at his father's pyramid, Khufu made a decision.
I need to build a pyramid to rival my father's. That will show how powerful I am.

Khufu met with his main advisor, called a vizier. He told the vizier of his plans.

I agree, my lord. You must build a pyramid just as your father did. However, you should make your pyramid the greatest the world has ever seen!

The vizier appointed an architect who drew plans for the new pyramid.

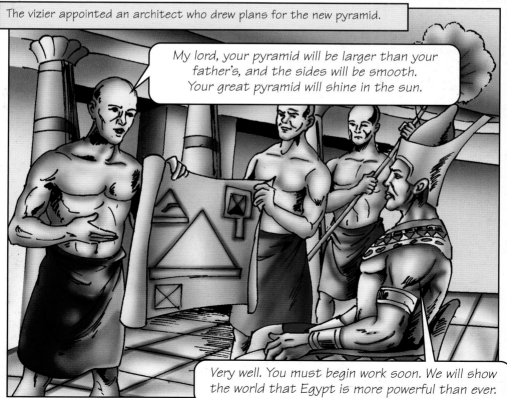

My lord, your pyramid will be larger than your father's, and the sides will be smooth. Your great pyramid will shine in the sun.

Very well. You must begin work soon. We will show the world that Egypt is more powerful than ever.

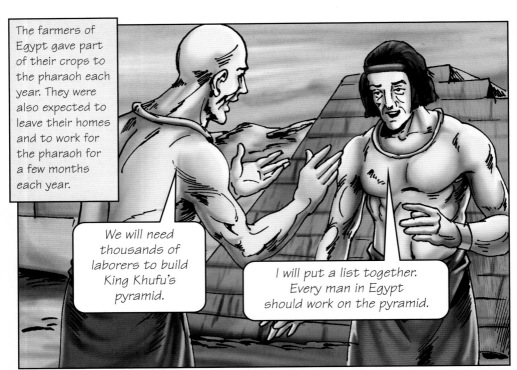

The farmers of Egypt gave part of their crops to the pharaoh each year. They were also expected to leave their homes and to work for the pharaoh for a few months each year.

We will need thousands of laborers to build King Khufu's pyramid.

I will put a list together. Every man in Egypt should work on the pyramid.

There were times when it was better for farmers to leave their land in order to work for the pharaoh. The vizier knew that the crops still had to be grown and harvested.

The floods have arrived. We'll have a good crop next year.

Yes, but while the flood waters cover our fields, we have little to do. We will probably have to work for the pharaoh.

Officials created lists of men who would help build the pyramid. They traveled from village to village to take the men to Giza to start building the pyramid.

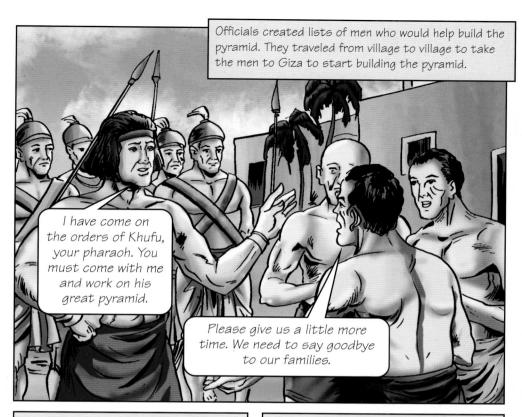

I have come on the orders of Khufu, your pharaoh. You must come with me and work on his great pyramid.

Please give us a little more time. We need to say goodbye to our families.

Many of the men who were taken to work at Giza had to leave for three months at a time.

Now, don't worry about me. It is only for three months, and I will be treated well.

I will pray to the gods for your safe return.

The men who worked on the building site were offered more than just food, shelter, and clothing.

This is a great privilege for us. If we help Khufu's journey to the afterlife, we will be allowed to make that journey, too.

Before the laborers could start building the pyramid, a site had to be chosen. It was decided that the pyramid would be built on the west side of the Nile. This was for both practical and religious reasons.

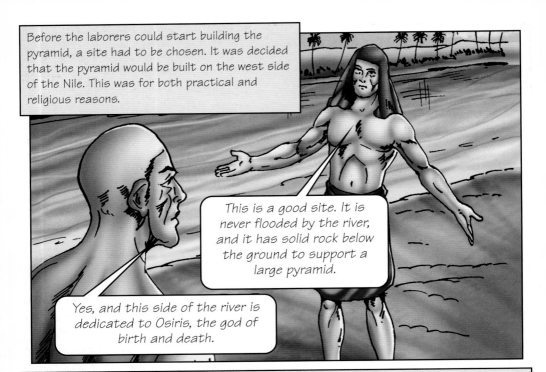

This is a good site. It is never flooded by the river, and it has solid rock below the ground to support a large pyramid.

Yes, and this side of the river is dedicated to Osiris, the god of birth and death.

The pyramid had to be built so that its four sides faced north, south, east, and west. The ancient Egyptians did not have a compass, so they relied on a priest to find north for them by looking up at the night sky.

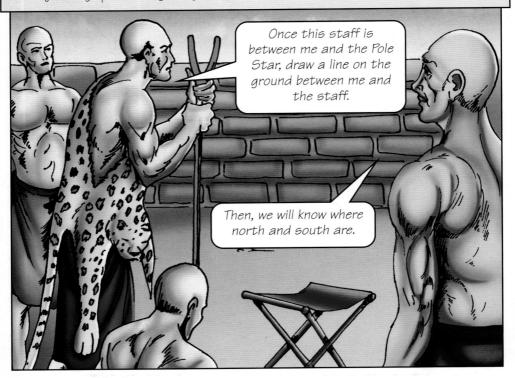

Once this staff is between me and the Pole Star, draw a line on the ground between me and the staff.

Then, we will know where north and south are.

Once the priest had determined the direction that the pyramid would be facing, the corners of the pyramid were marked. This was an important religious ceremony.

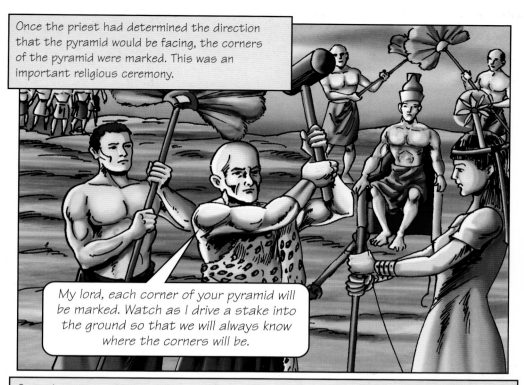

My lord, each corner of your pyramid will be marked. Watch as I drive a stake into the ground so that we will always know where the corners will be.

Once the ceremonies were over, work began on the pyramid. The first thing that had to be done, however, was to level the land and lay the foundation for the massive structure to rest on.

How many more of these rocks do we have to carry away?

Pull! Everybody pull together!

I don't know, but I'd rather be doing this than pulling those foundation stones. That's hard work.

FAST FACT About 4,000 men worked on the pyramid all year around.

The stone used for building the pyramid came from local quarries. The quarries had to be close to the river so that stone could easily be transported to the building site at Giza.

This stone will be good for the inside of the pyramid.

Yes, it will. But we must go to Tura for the limestone. We also need granite. That will have to come from far away.

The quarry needed skilled stonemasons who could cut the blocks of stone correctly. It was important that they worked closely with the architect.

The blocks of stone were cut out of the rock and then shaped to the site. Everything had to be done by hand.

I will need all the workers you can spare. We have many blocks of stone to carve out.

I will make sure that you have all of the men that you need.

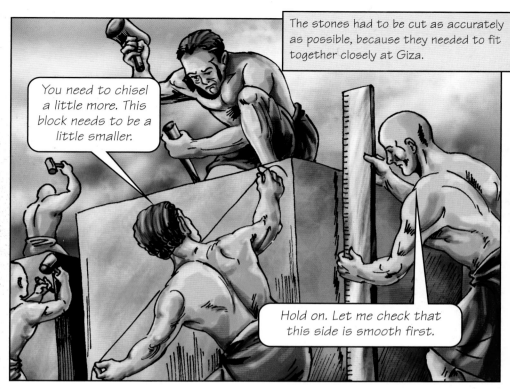

The stones had to be cut as accurately as possible, because they needed to fit together closely at Giza.

You need to chisel a little more. This block needs to be a little smaller.

Hold on. Let me check that this side is smooth first.

When a block of stone was the right size and smooth on all sides, it would be taken to the pyramid site at Giza .

You have to take your time with that. If you don't, then the block cannot be used.

At last, we've finished. You took your time getting it smooth.

Once all the rituals and preparations had been carried out at the pyramid site, workers began moving the huge stone blocks from the quarry. This was an exhausting task that used thousands of laborers.

Once the stones had been shaped and finished, they had to be transported to Giza. The stones were taken by boat down the Nile river. However, the quarry was not right next to the river, so the stones had be carried to the boats.

Come on, put your backs into it!

Uurgh! I'll never complain about farming again!

Once the blocks of stone reached the river, they had to be carefully lowered into the boat. The stones were so heavy that some of them slipped and fell on the waiting boats.

The stone's falling! Watch out below!

Once the stones were on the boats, they could then be transported down the river to Giza. Boats full of stone headed toward the building site, and empty boats went back to the quarry.

Slow down, this isn't a race! You'll tip us over if you go too fast!

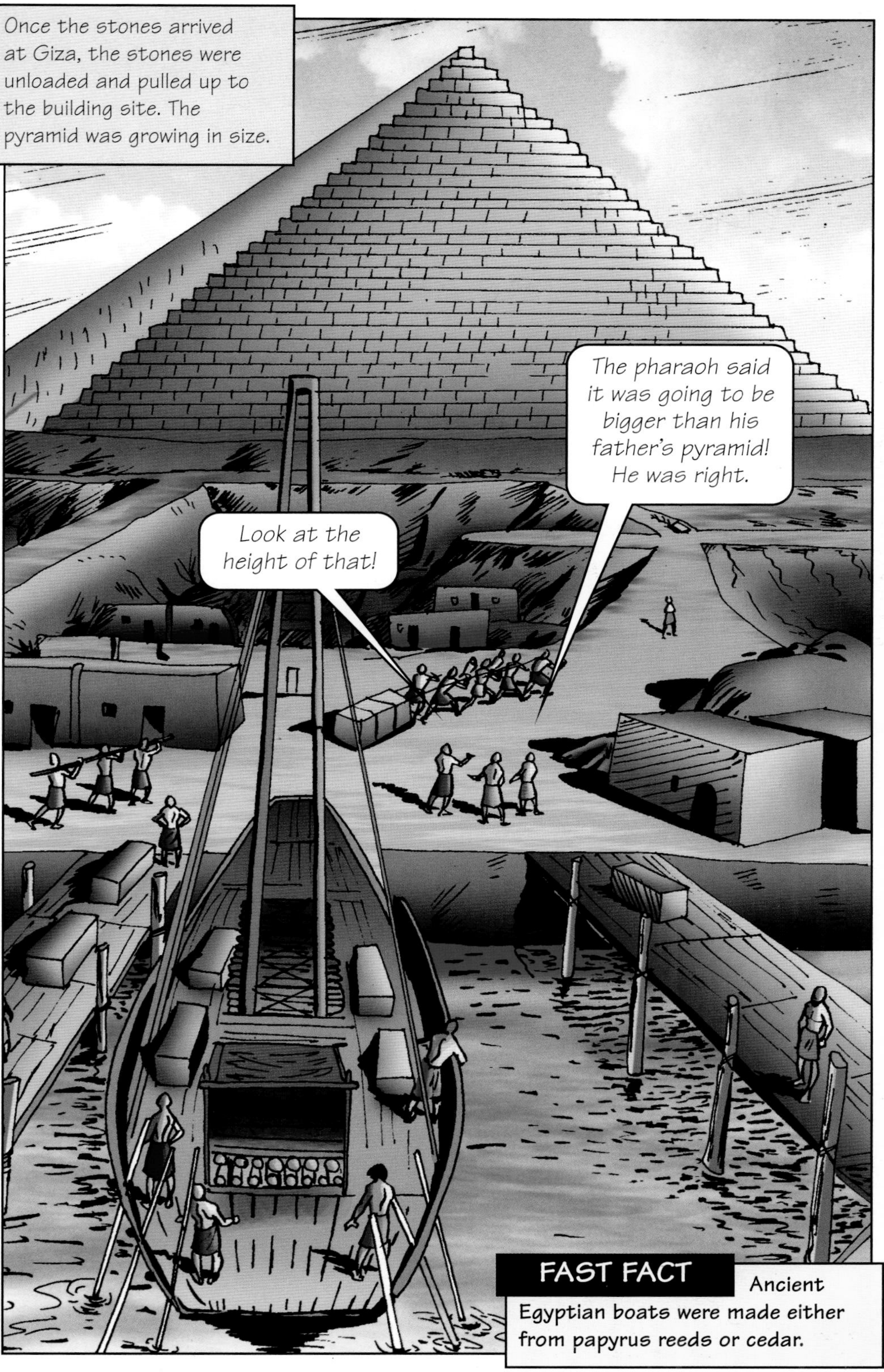
Once the stones arrived at Giza, the stones were unloaded and pulled up to the building site. The pyramid was growing in size.
The pharaoh said it was going to be bigger than his father's pyramid! He was right.
Look at the height of that!
FAST FACT
Ancient Egyptian boats were made either from papyrus reeds or cedar.

Khufu and his vizier visited the building site to check on the progress. It is believed that the pyramid took about 20 years to complete.

I can see that. I will have a pyramid that will make Egypt mightier still.

The work is going well, my lord.

No one is quite sure how the Egyptians raised the blocks of stone up the pyramid. Some historians believe that a spiral ramp was built around the outside of the pyramid so that the blocks could be pulled up. Others believe that one huge ramp was built at the side of the pyramid. The ramp then grew in height and length as each layer of the pyramid was added.

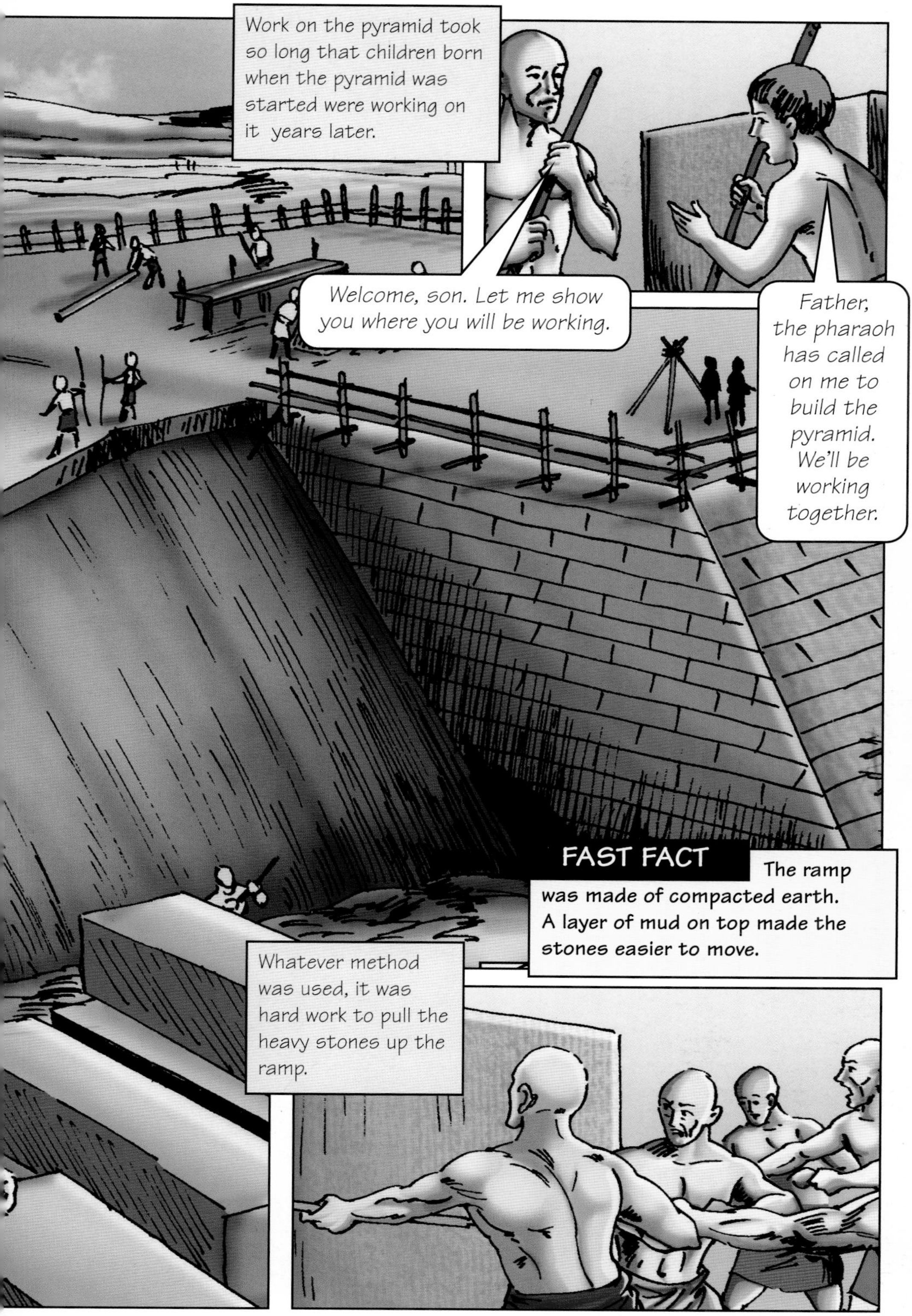
Work on the pyramid took so long that children born when the pyramid was started were working on it years later.
Welcome, son. Let me show you where you will be working.
Father, the pharaoh has called on me to build the pyramid. We'll be working together.
FAST FACT The ramp was made of compacted earth. A layer of mud on top made the stones easier to move.
Whatever method was used, it was hard work to pull the heavy stones up the ramp.

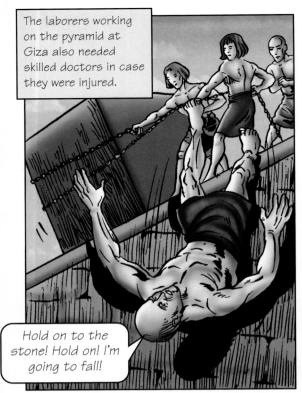

The laborers working on the pyramid at Giza also needed skilled doctors in case they were injured.

Hold on to the stone! Hold on! I'm going to fall!

Help me! I've broken my arm! Somebody help me!

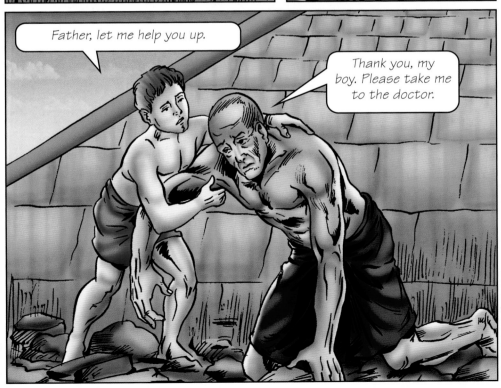

Father, let me help you up.

Thank you, my boy. Please take me to the doctor.

Doctor, my father has broken his arm.

Bring him inside.

Ancient Egyptian doctors were skilled. They used herbs as medicines and even knew how to fix broken bones, using splints to stabilize the bone.

I'm putting your arm in a splint. You will be out of work for a while.

Don't worry about me. My boy will take care of me.

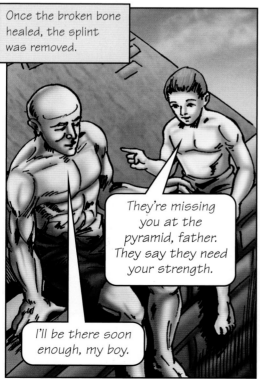

Once the broken bone healed, the splint was removed.

They're missing you at the pyramid, father. They say they need your strength.

I'll be there soon enough, my boy.

Once the bone was fully healed, the worker was back at work on the pyramid.

All together now! Pull!

FAST FACT Workers on the pyramid were divided into gangs. They had names like the *Western Gang* and the *Green Gang*.

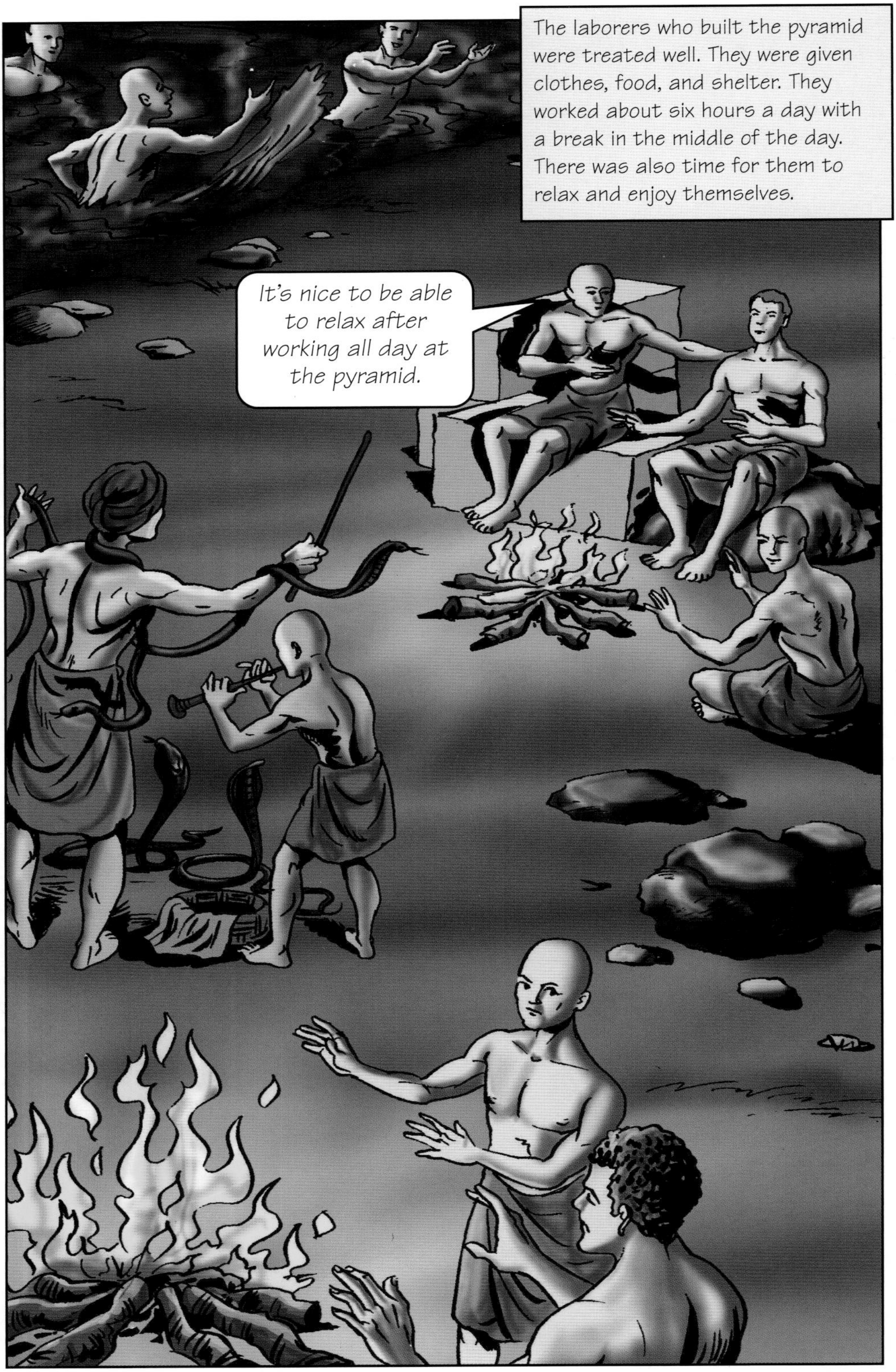
The laborers who built the pyramid were treated well. They were given clothes, food, and shelter. They worked about six hours a day with a break in the middle of the day. There was also time for them to relax and enjoy themselves.
It's nice to be able to relax after working all day at the pyramid.

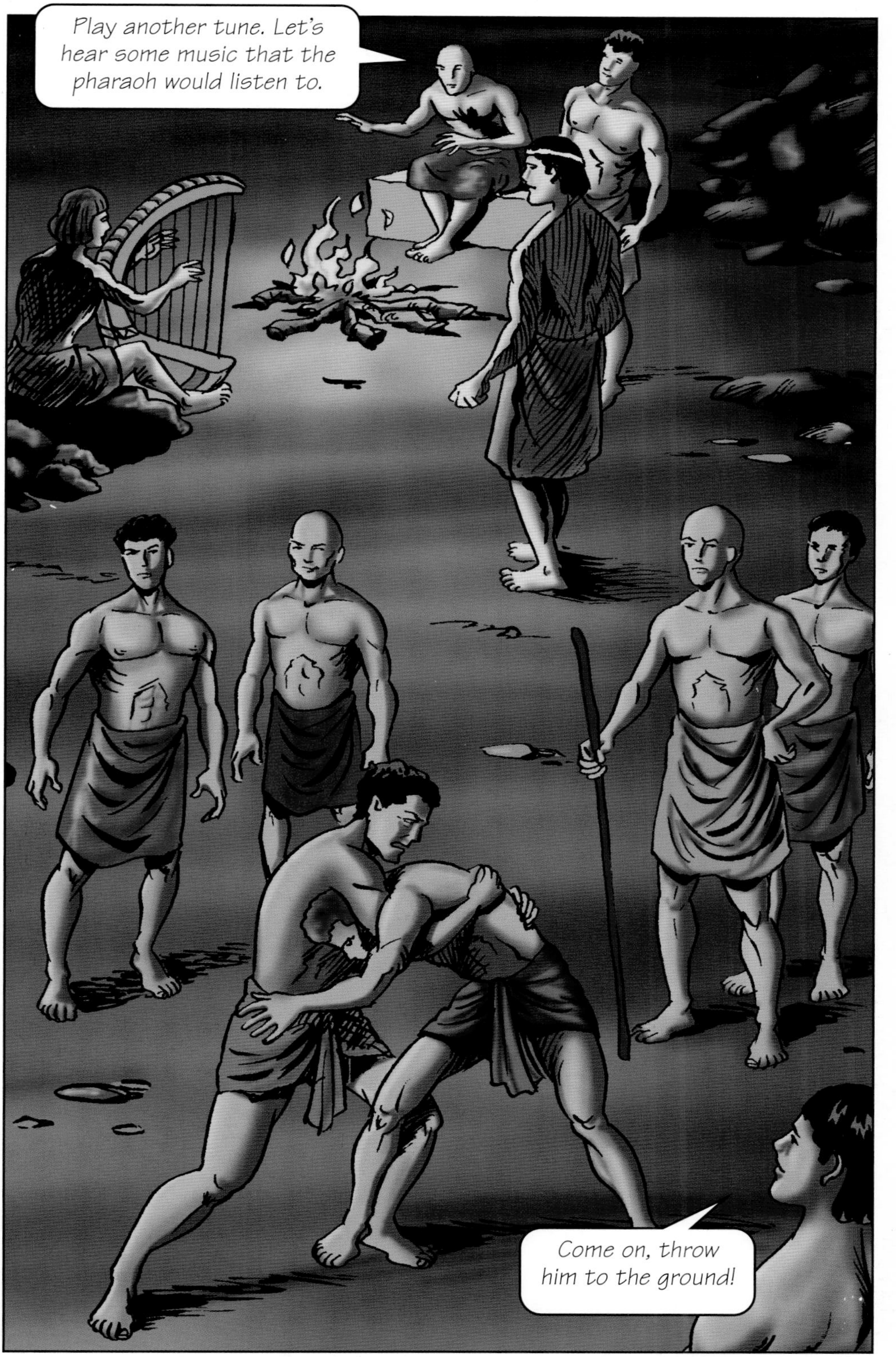
Play another tune. Let's hear some music that the pharaoh would listen to.
Come on, throw him to the ground!

The vizier and the architect needed to make sure that the chambers inside the pyramid were also built correctly.

We must stop building the pyramid walls for a while. We need to build the chambers inside.

Then, we will need the granite from Aswan.

THE GREAT PYRAMID

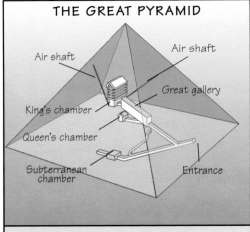

Air shaft

Air shaft

King's chamber

Great gallery

Queen's chamber

Subterranean chamber

Entrance

The network of passages inside the pyramid included walkways and airshafts leading to the burial chambers.

The red granite blocks used to line the walls of the chamber were brought from the quarry at Aswan. Granite is a heavy stone that is very difficult to shape.

Careful with that block. We have to keep it in one piece.

Don't forget this is the floor. These granite blocks need to be as smooth as possible.

The door to the main chamber in the pyramid was also made of granite.
The door had to be pulled into an upright position and pulled to the right place.

Sometimes, mistakes were made, and new ways had to be found to solve these problems.

I've got the block steady. Ready? Pull together!

Pull! Pull!

My lord, the roof of the chamber will not be strong enough to bear the weight of the pyramid.

Then you will have to find a way to make it stronger.

To make the chamber roof strong enough, we will have to put five roofs on top of each other.

The granite chambers were completed, and the architect showed the vizier what had been built.

The pharaoh will be very pleased. This is a tomb worthy of him and his family.

Five roofs? That's five granite slabs. Do you know how heavy those blocks are?

FAST FACT The airshafts leading from the burial chambers point toward constellations of stars in the night sky.

Once the inside of the pyramid was complete, the white limestone blocks needed to be put on the outside.

We are getting close to finishing the pyramid. Limestone will make it shine in the sun.

Then, bring in the limestone from Tura. We must begin immediately.

The limestone blocks had to be lifted into place in the same way as the other blocks. However, each of these stones also had to be cut at the same angle and carefully placed next to each other.

Careful! These limsetone blocks need to be placed perfectly!

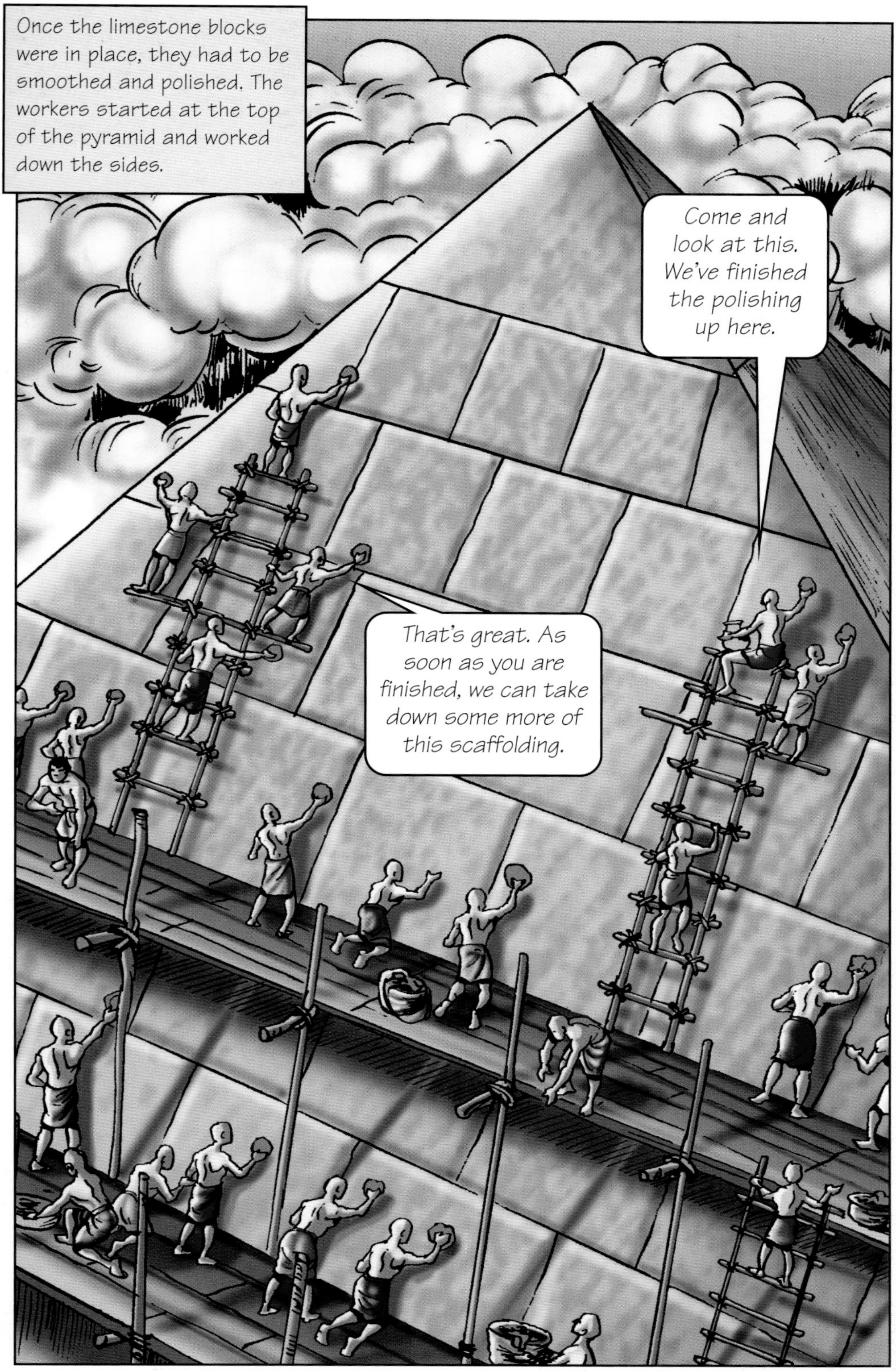
Once the limestone blocks were in place, they had to be smoothed and polished. The workers started at the top of the pyramid and worked down the sides.
Come and look at this. We've finished the polishing up here.
That's great. As soon as you are finished, we can take down some more of this scaffolding.

The walls of the chambers were painted and decorated. It was believed that these paintings had magical powers that would help the pharaoh in the afterlife.

Mix that plaster well, my boy. We have to make these walls smooth before they can be painted.

Once the plaster was dry, a grid of red lines was painted on the wall.

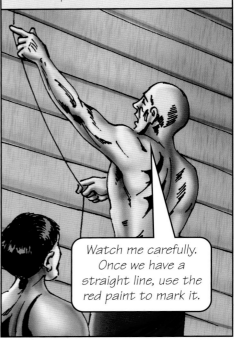

Watch me carefully. Once we have a straight line, use the red paint to mark it.

An artist also drew the outlines of the images using red paint.

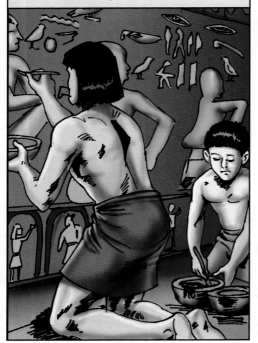

Corrections were then made in black paint.

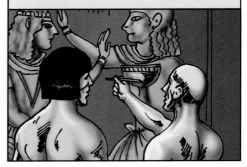

Once the outlines were done, the images were painted using different colors.

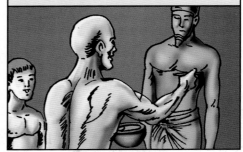

Details, such as the eyes and mouth, were added.

I need some more blue paint over here, son.

Coming! I've just finished mixing it.

The finished chamber was covered with bright and colorful pictures.

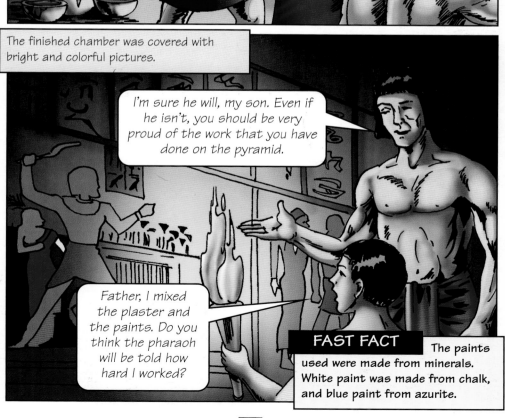

I'm sure he will, my son. Even if he isn't, you should be very proud of the work that you have done on the pyramid.

Father, I mixed the plaster and the paints. Do you think the pharaoh will be told how hard I worked?

FAST FACT The paints used were made from minerals. White paint was made from chalk, and blue paint from azurite.

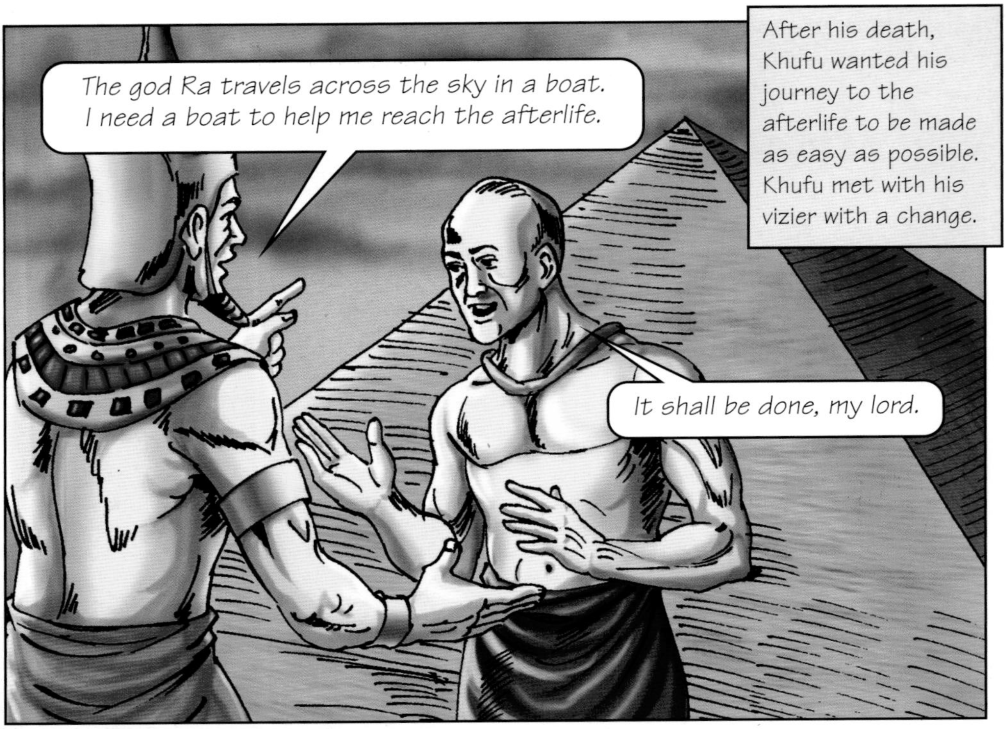
After his death, Khufu wanted his journey to the afterlife to be made as easy as possible. Khufu met with his vizier with a change.
The god Ra travels across the sky in a boat. I need a boat to help me reach the afterlife.
It shall be done, my lord.

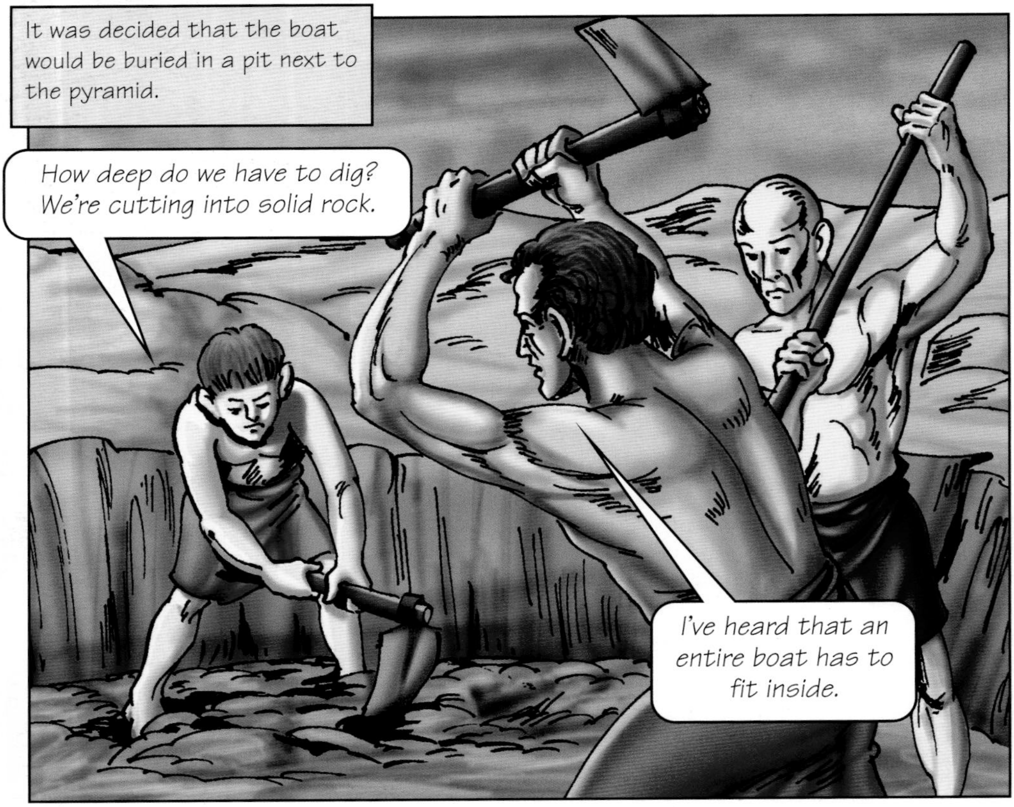
It was decided that the boat would be buried in a pit next to the pyramid.
How deep do we have to dig? We're cutting into solid rock.
I've heard that an entire boat has to fit inside.

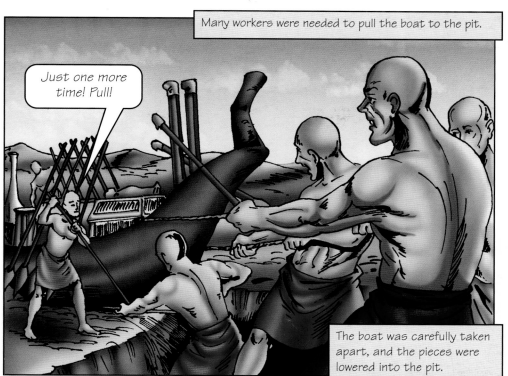

Many workers were needed to pull the boat to the pit.

Just one more time! Pull!

The boat was carefully taken apart, and the pieces were lowered into the pit.

Once the slabs are all in place, cover it under the sand. Nobody must know this is here.

Once all of the pieces of the boat were in the pit, it was covered with stone slabs and sand to protect it from grave robbers.

FAST FACT   The boat was 150 feet long. It was broken into 1,224 separate pieces to be buried.

DEATH OF A PHARAOH

The Great Pyramid was built not just as a symbol of Egypt's power, but also as a tomb for Khufu and his family. When Khufu died in 2566 B.C., preparations began to place his body in the King's Chamber.

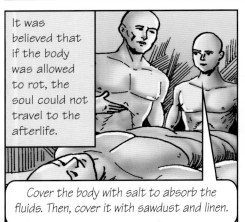

It was believed that if the body was allowed to rot, the soul could not travel to the afterlife.

Cover the body with salt to absorb the fluids. Then, cover it with sawdust and linen.

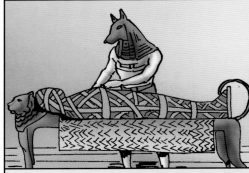

After Khufu's body was dried, it was wrapped in linen bandages. This was done by an embalmer dressed as the god Anubis.

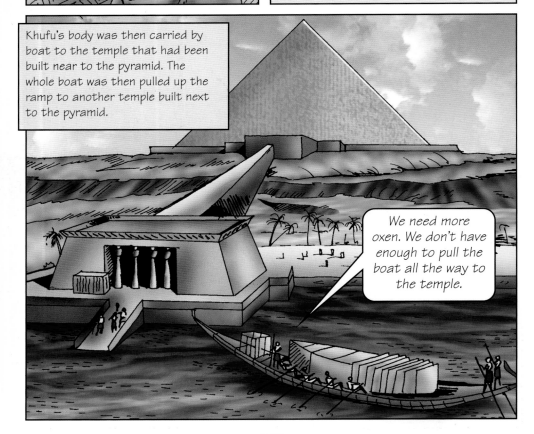

Khufu's body was then carried by boat to the temple that had been built near to the pyramid. The whole boat was then pulled up the ramp to another temple built next to the pyramid.

We need more oxen. We don't have enough to pull the boat all the way to the temple.

38

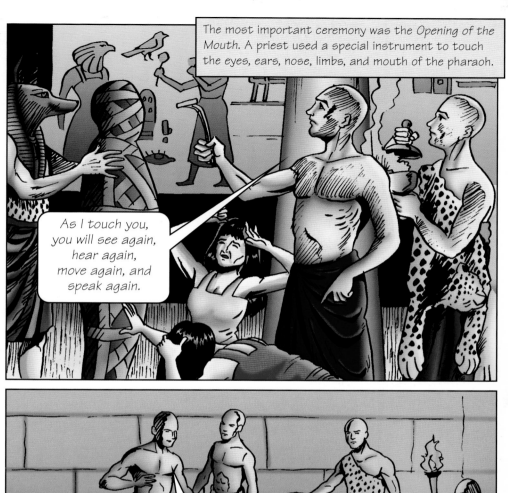

The most important ceremony was the *Opening of the Mouth*. A priest used a special instrument to touch the eyes, ears, nose, limbs, and mouth of the pharaoh.

As I touch you, you will see again, hear again, move again, and speak again.

Be sure that the chamber is sealed first. Then, we can leave by climbing along one of the tunnels.

Once all of these ceremonies were finished, Khufu's body was taken to the burial chamber inside the pyramid. It was placed inside a stone sarcophagus, and everybody left the chamber.

FAST FACT
Khufu's sarcophagus must have been put in when the chamber was built. It was too big to fit through the Grand Gallery.

No matter how well the pyramid had been built, the treasures inside the chambers were a great temptation for tomb robbers. By 1000 B.C., almost every pyramid in Egypt had been robbed.

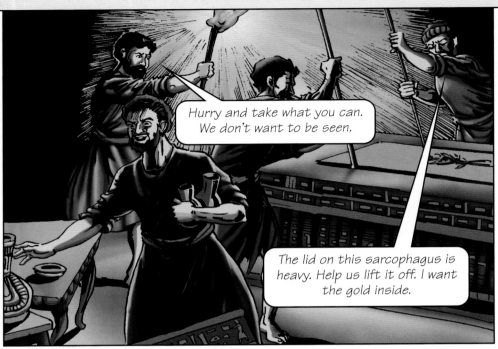

In A.D. 641, Muslim invaders conquered Egypt. They were fascinated by these mysterious buildings.

The Muslim rulers found no treasure. However, in A.D. 969, they decided to build a new capital city at Cairo. They pulled off the limestone blocks to use as building material.

Carry on with your work. We will make our new city as glorious as these pyramids once were.

The pyramids today no longer look much like they did when they were built. Only the top of the Khufu's great pyramid still has the original limestone casing.

Just take a picture. You know we're not allowed to take any of the stones from the pyramid.

This is what the group of pyramids built by Khufu and other pharaohs look like today. The pyramid on the left was built by Khufu's son, Khafre. The small pyramid on the right is the Queen's Pyramid. The buildings in front are the remains of the worker's houses.

This picture shows the chambers and galleries inside the pyramid. There are also a number escape paths and unfinished passages in the pyramid.

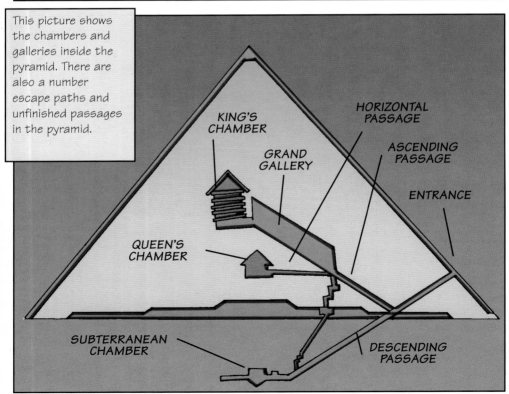

KING'S CHAMBER

GRAND GALLERY

HORIZONTAL PASSAGE

ASCENDING PASSAGE

ENTRANCE

QUEEN'S CHAMBER

SUBTERRANEAN CHAMBER

DESCENDING PASSAGE

This shows one of the passages that were built. They were very narrow and were meant to keep tomb robbers out.

This is the Queen's Chamber. It was too narrow for a body and was probably meant to hold a statue.

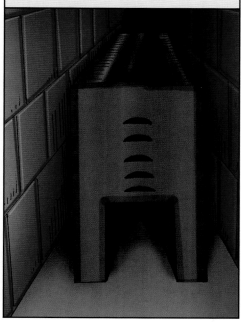

The Grand Gallery led to the King's Chamber. It was much bigger than all of the other galleries.

The King's Chamber measuree 33 x 16 x 16 feet. Khufu was placed in a sarcophagus at the west end.

TIMELINE OF ANCIENT EGYPT

Ancient Egypt was one of the largest and greatest civilizations the world has ever known. Its ancient monuments, including the mighty pyramids, still attract thousands of visitors every day. The Great Pyramid of Giza, built by Pharaoh Khufu, is the most famous of all. Ancient Egypt's history is filled with times of peace and war.

5000 B.C.: *The Nile Valley is first settled and farming begins.*

3000 B.C.: *The two kingdoms of Upper and Lower Egypt are united by King Narmer.*

2700 B.C.: *The first pyramid is built by King Djoser. The Old Kingdom of Ancient Egypt begins.*

2500 B.C.: *King Sneferu begins the fourth dynasty of the Old Kingdom.*

2465 B.C.: *King Sneferu dies and Khufu becomes the new pharaoh.*

2435 B.C.: *Khufu dies and is buried in the Great Pyramid.*

2100 B.C.: *The First Intermediate Period begins. For the next hundred years, Egypt suffers from civil wars and famine.*

2000 B.C.: *During the Middle Kingdom, Egypt is reunited by a prince of Thebes.*

1700 B.C.: *The Hyksos invade and conquer much of Egypt.*

1650–1550 B.C.: *The Second Intermediate Period.*

1550 B.C.: *The Hyksos are driven out, and Egypt begins the New Kingdom.*

1504–1492 B.C.: *Reign of Pharaoh Tutmosis I. He is the first Egyptian ruler to have a tomb in the Valley of the Kings.*

1336–1327 B.C.: *The famous Tutankhamun is pharaoh.*

1279–1213 B.C.: *Under the reign of Ramesses II, the temple at Abu Simbel is built.*

1067–747 B.C. *The Third Intermediate Period.*

747–332 B.C. *The Late Period.*

525–404 B.C.: *Egypt is invaded and becomes part of the Persian Empire. When the Persians are defeated, the country returns to Egyptian rule.*

450 B.C.: *The Greek traveler and historian Herodotus visits Egypt.*

332 B.C.–A.D. 395: *The Greek-Roman period.*

343–332 B.C.: *Second invasion by Persia.*

332–30 B.C.: *Egypt is conquered by Alexander the Great and the Persians are removed from power.*

30 B.C.–A.D. 641: *Egypt becomes part of the Roman and Byzantine Empires. Much of the country is converted to Christianity.*

A.D. 641: *Egypt is conquered by the Muslims.*

A.D. 969: *The limestone blocks of the Great Pyramid are removed to help build the city of Cairo.*

1. *The Great Pyramid is 482 feet high.*

2. *The base of the Great Pyramid is just over 755 feet wide.*

3. *The pyramids were believed to be staircases to heaven and were the resting place of the very rich and rulers.*

4. *The pyramids were built in a triangular shape so the sun always shone on one side.*

5. *The Great Pyramid has 200 layers of stone from top to bottom.*

6. *There were very few slaves in Egypt, and only a few of them were used in the building of the pyramids.*

7. *There are more than 80 pyramids in Egypt. Most of them are in ruins, but a few survive. There are also a few surviving temples, such as the two at Abu Simbel.*

8. *Cats were popular pets in ancient Egypt. After they died, they were often mummified and put into coffins.*

9. *It took about two weeks for Khufu's body to be properly wrapped with linen and mummified.*

10. *The average block of stone on the Great Pyramid weighed about 2.5 tons. Some of the stones weighed over 15 tons.*

11. *When Khufu died, professional mourners were hired to express the whole country's sorrow by singing.*

12. *Khufu's internal organs, like the heart and lungs, were mummified separately and placed in jars.*

13. *The Egyptians called the afterlife the* Field of Reeds. *It was a place where the sun always shone and crops were always plentiful.*

14. *The paint used to decorate the chambers in the pyramid were so expensive that they were locked away every night.*

15. *The tombs of the ancient pharaohs were protected by curses. In order to make sure dead pharaohs were safe in the afterlife, curses were made that said anyone who defiled a pharaoh's tomb would die.*

16. *Lord Carnarvon and his team, who discovered King Tut's tomb, had a series of bad experiences after opening King Tut's tomb.*

17. *Lord Carnarvon himself died just five months after his great discovery from a mosquito bite.*

18. *Modern archaeologists believe that mold growing inside the tombs were responsible for the many deaths suffered by Egyptologists, not curses.*

GLOSSARY

Afterlife: *The Egyptian belief that there is a new life after death. It was known to the Egyptians as the* Next World.

Anubis: *The guardian of the dead and the god of embalming.*

Architect: *Someone who designs buildings and oversees them being built.*

Archeologists: *People who study history by studying ancient objects.*

Capstone: *The pointed stone placed at the top of a pyramid.*

Canopic jars: *Jars that were used to hold mummified internal organs.*

Casing blocks: *Finely cut and polished blocks that form the outer layer of the pyramid.*

Cataract: *A place where outcrops of rock distrub the flow of the Nile. There are six in the Nile.*

Causeway: *A raised path or road.*

Cheops: *Another name for Khufu.*

Civilization: *A culture and its people.*

Dynasty: *A family of rulers. Egypt had 31 dynasties.*

Egyptology: *The study of ancient Egypt.*

Embalmer: *Someone who preserves a dead body against decay.*

Fertile: *Land that is good for farming.*

Hathor: *One of Egypt's oldest and most powerful goddesses. Seen as a mother who protects her worshippers in this world and the next. Her sacred animal is a cow.*

Horus: *The god of the sky and kingship. One of Egypt's most ancient gods, his sacred animal is the falcon.*

Inundation: *A technical name for an annual flood that people depended on to grow food.*

Khnum: *God of the First Cataract, controller of the Nile. He created people's bodies and spirits on a potter's wheel. (see* **Cataract***)*

Mortuary temple: *The temple built against the side of a pyramid. The priests were supposed to make daily offerings to the dead king's spirit for all eternity.*

Mummification: *The Egyptian method of preserving a body after death.*

Nubia: *An important trading country south of Egypt.*

Opening of the Mouth: *A ceremony that gives a dead person the power to speak, breath, feel, and move again.*

Osiris: *God of the dead and ruler of the underworld. He became one of Egypt's most popular deities.*

Papyrus: *Type of reed plant used to make many things, including parchment.*

Pharaoh: *A word formed from the two words* par *and* aa. *It means* great house. *It was a respectful way of referring to the Egyptian king.*

Portcullis: *A gate or door that can be closed by sliding it down.*

Quarry: *A place where blocks of stone are cut out and shaped.*

Ra: *The sun god and one of Egypt's most important deities. His main temple was at Heliopolis, north of Memphis.*

Sarcophagus: *A stone coffin. The body was placed in a wooden coffin and then put into a sacrophagus.*

Sphinx: *A stone figure that has a human head and the body of a lion. The one at Giza is the most famous, but there are other, smaller ones.*

Stela: *An upright slab of stone or wood with inscriptions carved or written on it. The inscriptions are usually religious and record a special event.*

Thoth: *God of wisdom and medicine.*

Tomb: *A place where someone's body is buried.*

Two lands: *Term used to show that Egypt started off as two separate kingdoms: Upper (southern) and Lower (northern) Egypt.*

Valley temple: *A temple in a pyramid complex. It stood where the valley met the desert.*

Vizier: *The pharaoh's most important adviser.*

Underworld: *Another realm inhabited by the dead. Everyday. the god Ra had to sail through the underworld to ensure the Sun rose in the morning.*

INDEX

Abu Simbel 44, 45
afterlife 17, 34, 36, 45, 46
airshafts 30, 31
Anubis 38, 46
archeologists 45, 46
architect 15, 20, 30–31, 46
Aswan 30
boats 22–23, 36–37, 38
Cairo 41, 44
Carnarvon, Lord 45
cats 45
chambers 30–31, 34–35
curses 45
death 13, 38–39
Djoser 6, 44
doctors 26–27
dynasties 10, 46
Egypt 4–7, 44
embalmer 38, 46
farmers and farming 6–7, 16–17
floods 5, 6, 9, 16
gangs 27
gods and goddesses 8–9
    Anubis 38, 46
    Hathor 12, 46
    Horus 9, 46
    Khnum 9, 46
    Osiris 18, 47
    Ra 36, 47
    Thoth 9, 12, 47
Grand Gallery 43
granite 20, 30–31
Hathor 12, 46
Hetepheres 2, 10
Horus 9, 46
injuries 26–27
Khafre 42
Khnum 9, 46
Khufu 2, 8–15, 36–39, 43, 44, 45
King's Chamber 43
limestone 20, 32–33, 44
Meritetes 2, 12

monkeys 9
mummification 45, 46, 47
Muslim invaders 40–41, 44
Narmer 2, 5, 44
Nile 4, 5, 18, 22, 44
Opening of the Mouth ceremony 39, 47
Osiris 18, 47
paint and paintings 34–35, 45
papyrus 23, 47
passages 30, 42
pharaohs 8–13, 47
    Khufu 2, 8–15, 36–39, 43, 44, 45
    Narmer 2, 5, 44
    Sneferu 2, 10–13, 44
    Tutankhamun 44, 45
    Tutmosis I 44
polishing 33
priests 18, 39
quarries 20, 47
queens 2, 10, 12
Queen's Chamber 30, 42, 43
Ra 36, 47
ramps 24–25
relaxation 28–29
religious ceremonies 8–9, 10, 12, 19, 39
robbers 40, 42
roofs 31
sarcophagus 39, 47
slaves 45
smoothing 21, 33
Sneferu 2, 10–13, 44
stone and stonemasons 20–23, 45
Thoth 9, 12, 47
transport 22–23
Tutankhamun 44, 45
Tutmosis I 44
vizier 15, 24, 30–31, 36, 47
wall paintings 34–35